# Fairy Tale Twists

## Three Magic Mice

Written by Katie Dale
Illustrated by Matt Buckingham

ORCHARD

Far off, in a distant land,
there stood a mansion, tall and grand.

The home of Cinders, Red and Bella,
and, beneath them, in the cellar…

In a hole lived three blind mice –
three brothers, to be quite precise.

They led a rather risky life,
and spent their days avoiding strife,
by dodging pots, and bubbling vats…

and knives and forks and traps and cats…

and Betty-Sue, the farmer's wife,
who chased the rodents with a knife!

Somehow they always got away,
that is, until one fateful day…
behind the fridge the mice got stuck!
It seemed they had run out of luck!

When suddenly a **FLASH** of light
turned everything a blinding white!
The three mice started feeling strange –
they felt themselves begin to change…

"What's happening to us?" One cried.
"Hey! I can see!" Mouse Three replied.

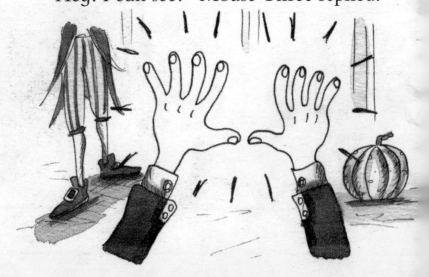

'My claws have gone!" exclaimed Mouse Two.

'Look – I've got hands! With fingers too!

Hey, we're not rodents any more!

We've got two feet instead of four!"

A fairy stepped into the light.
"You're men!" she smiled, "for just one night.
And in return, all that I ask
is that you do one simple task…"

Outside they found a horse and coach
(made from a pumpkin and cockroach).
"Take Cinders to the ball tonight,
and bring her home before midnight."

"Of course! No prob!" the brothers cried.
They dropped off Cinders right outside.
"Let's go!" grinned One. "For after all,
we're men tonight — let's have a ball!"

They danced until it made their knees ache,

then they spotted pies – and
**CHEESEcake!**

They ate all night, it seemed like heaven,
till the clock chimed half-eleven…
"*Must* we turn to mice again!"
wailed Brother One. "Can't we stay men?"

"*I* know!" cried the second brother.
"We'll *hide* from our Fairy Godmother!
If she can't find us, she can never
change us – we'll be men forever!"

But you should never cross a fairy –
when they're angry they get SCARY!
"If they don't want to be three mice –"
she flicked her wand – "they'll pay
   the price!"

Meanwhile, not so far away,
the brothers had a lovely day,
till One spotted a **WANTED** sign.
"I recognise that face – it's mine!"

"Me too! It's all of us!" cried Two.

"Whatever are we going to do?"

"Calm down," said Three. "We'll just
   lie low."

But then a goatherd stopped. "Hello!
You're the fellas up for ransom!"

"Pah!" laughed Three. "We're not
   that handsome!"

"Yes, we are!" his brother cried.

"*Quick!*" hissed Brother Three. "Let's
    hide!"

They darted in amongst the herd,
then something very strange occurred…

The brothers all began to bleat
then *hooves* grew on their hands and feet!

Beards appeared round all their throats,
as they turned into billy goats!

"What's happening to us?" wailed Two.
"First we're men, and now goats too!"
"At least now anyone who spies us
Will not ever recognise us!"
"Now we're safe!" cried Brother Three.
"Hurray!" the brothers skipped in glee.

But as they crossed a gushing stream
A TROLL let out an angry scream!
"Who made my roof shake? Answer me!
I"ll eat the culprit for my tea!"
"Not me!" yelped One. "I'm much too light
to satisfy your appetite!"

"I'm far too small!" cried Two. "Not me!"

"It was I!" said Brother Three.

Troll grinned, for Three was plump and tall
– the biggest billy goat of all!

The troll rushed over, but instead...
Three **KICKED** the troll over his head!

The brothers quickly ran away,
And hid behind some bales of hay.

But then they started feeling weird –
their horns and beards disappeared!

A snout replaced each brother's nose,
and trotters grew upon their toes!

"We've turned to pigs!" Two cried.
  "But why?"
"Look!" said Three. "We're in a sty!
We must change to whatever's close!"
"Yucky!" One whined. "Pigs are gross!"

Three grinned. "The troll was right
  behind us,
but now we've changed he'll never find us!"
"Yippee," cried One. "But I feel sick.
I need to leave this sty – and quick!"

So off they went, and all three pigs
found homes of straw, and bricks, and twigs.

But then a wolf came into town,
and blew the first pig's home right down!

"Help!" cried One as Wolf gave chase
He hurried to his brother's place...

Which fell down too! The frightened pigs
then sprinted to their brother's digs.
But still the wolf was on their heels,
hungry for two piggy meals!

But just as he climbed up the wall...
The woodsman came to save them all!

That night the brothers held a meeting.
"History keeps on repeating –
every day we run and flee,
it can't go on!" cried Brother Three.
"We need to change to something scary –
something big, and fierce and hairy."

"Witch!" cried Two.

"Good choice," said One.

"No – look!" yelled Two. "Behind you –
**RUN!**"

The pigs jumped up and fled in fright,
running blindly through the night,
until they tripped and slipped and **thwack!**
They hit their heads and all went black.

When One woke up he said his prayers...

For everywhere he looked were **BEARS**
about to have their picnic tea!

"Oh no!" he cried. "Please don't eat me!"
Two bears beside him winked. "That's daft!
Eat our own brother? Ha!" they laughed.

One stared. It simply couldn't be!
The bears were Brothers Two and Three!
He looked down – all his feet were paws!
Instead of trotters he had claws!

They danced and laughed without a care –
for who would ever hunt a bear?

But then one morning they were shocked
to find their cottage door unlocked…
They stepped inside. The house was
    trashed –
the fridge was bare, a chair was smashed.

Then overhead a floorboard creaked.
"There's someone up there!" Bear One
  squeaked.
They crept upstairs. "She's in my bed!"
A girl jumped out, and then she fled.

"Who was that?" the first bear cried.

"A thief!" the second bear replied.

"No, she's a warning," Bear Three
   sighed.

"To show us there's nowhere to hide."

"I know who sent her," said his brother.
"It must have been Fairy Godmother.
Ever since we disobeyed,
running is the price we've paid."

Just then, there came a flash of light –
the fairy re-appeared. "You're right!
You can run, and you can flee,
but you can never hide from me!
*Now all change back!*" the fairy cursed.
"*Return to how you were at first!
And once you're how you were before
STAY that way forever more!*"

The room went spinning in a blur…

the bears' ears shrank, they lost their fur…

they felt themselves reduce in size…

but when they opened up their eyes…

they got a very big **surprise!**

For they were *boys* instead of mice!

Princes, to be quite precise!

The fairy gasped. "What's going on?"
Just then the king rushed in.

"Prince John!"

He hurried over with the queen.
"Prince Mark! Prince Luke! Where have
you been?"

The brothers stared at one another.
Brother Three gasped, "Father? Mother?"

"My darling sons, don't you remember?
Years ago, one dark December,
we turned an old hag from our door,
even though the rain did pour."

The fairy screamed, "But not for long!
Each one of you has done me wrong!"
"*You're* the hag!" the old king cried.
"I'm sorry I shut you outside!"

"You're *sorry*?" Fairy sneered. "That's nice.
You still deserve to pay the price!
*Turn the brothers back to mice!*"
She flicked her wand…but nothing stirred.
The fairy glowered. "How absurd!"

"No, it's your spell!" cried Brother Three.
"You said, *Stay as you used to be.*
We *cannot* change – ever again!
We'll live forever more as men!"
The fairy glared as they all cheered,
then flicked her wand and disappeared.

And evermore, the princes three
rejoiced that they were home and free
(but still loved eating cheese for tea!)

# Fairy Tale Twists

### Written by Katie Dale
### Illustrated by Matt Buckingham

All priced at £4.99

Orchard Books are available from all good bookshops,
or can be ordered from our website, www.orchardbooks.co.uk,
or telephone 01235 827702, or fax 01235 827703.